HIEROGLYPHIC TALES

HIEROGLYPHIC TALES

HORACE WALPOLE

ILLUSTRATED BY JILL MCELMURRY

Mercury House ◆ San Francisco

Published in the United States
by Mercury House
San Francisco, California

"The Bird's Nest" is reprinted from A. Dayle Wallace, "Two Unpublished Fairy Tales by Horace Walpole" in *Horace Walpole: Writer, Politician, Connoisseur,* ed. Warren Hunting Smith (New Haven and London: Yale University Press, copyright © 1967). pp. 250–252; reprinted by permission of Yale University Press.

United States Constitution, First Amendment: Congress shall make no law respecting an establishment of religion, or prohibiting the free exercise thereof; or abridging the freedom of speech, or of the press; or the right of the people peaceably to assemble, and to petition the Government for a redress of grievances.

Cover and interior art by Jill McElmurry
Cover and text design by Sharon Smith

Printed on acid-free paper. Manufactured in the United States of America.

Library of Congress Cataloging-in-Publication Data

Walpole, Horace, 1717–1797.
   Hieroglyphic tales / Horace Walpole.
     p.   cm.
   ISBN 1-56279-049-8
     1. Fantastic fiction, English. I. Title.
   PR3757.W2H5 1993
   823´.6—dc20

                                    93-12723
                                       CIP

5   4   3   2   1

CONTENTS

EDITOR'S NOTE:
A HORACE READING

MOUSEBENDER: I was sitting in the public library in Thurmond Street just now, skimming through *Rogue Herries* by Horace Walpole, when suddenly I came over all peckish.

WENSLEYDALE: Peckish, sir?

MOUSEBENDER: Esurient.

WENSLEYDALE: Eh?

MOUSEBENDER: Eee, I were all 'ungry, like!

WENSLEYDALE: Oh, hungry.

MOUSEBENDER: In a nutshell. So I thought to myself "a little fermented curd will do the trick." So I curtailed my Walpolling activities, sallied forth and infiltrated your place of purveyance to negotiate the vending of some cheesy comestibles.

WENSLEYDALE: Come again?

MOUSEBENDER: I want to buy some cheese!

—"Monty Python's Flying Circus"

Not a tribute to Horace Walpole exactly. Yet the eighteenth-century earl would probably not have felt out of place in this sketch, for the Pythons continue a peculiar strain of British tradition distinguished by absurdity, ridicule, wordplay, wit, wickedness, and plain madness (not to mention cheesiness) that unquestionably reached one of its peaks in these extraordinary (and virtually unknown, even in England) *Hieroglyphic Tales*.

In a word: fermented curd. Herewith a few field notes for going Walpolling.

✦ ✦ ✦

He was about as odd as you would expect.

He lived (comfortably, thanks to a variety of sinecures—his father, Robert, had been prime minister of England under King George I) in a house on the banks of the Thames near Twickenham; he called the house Strawberry Hill and made it into "a little Gothic castle" decked out with fake pinnacles, battlements, ornamental facades, and gargoyles of lath and plaster

and crammed to overflowing with all manner of antiquities, curiosities, and ob-
jets d'art. Toward the end of his life and for some time thereafter (at least
until a famous auction of its contents in 1842), Strawberry Hill was a tourist
attraction. According to his memorandum book, Walpole personally ushered
some four thousand visitors through it (complaining all the while of the in-
convenience). Often criticized as a cheap, slipshod sham, it has also been
lauded as a "subjunctive" edifice, an "architecture of the 'as if,' "[1] and as a creation that overturns conventional "rigid and stately rules of architecture."[2]

Besides being an extremely prolific writer ("When will it end?" wrote a
reviewer in 1851 of Walpole's posthumous letters, well before they had attained
their present mass of forty-eight volumes), he was a publisher (depending on
your point of view, his publishing was "simple and restrained"[3] or character-
ized by "rather indifferent printing;"[4] in any case, his Strawberry Hill Press
stands as the first privately held printing press in England). Yet Horace
Walpole, publisher, had a peculiar attitude to being published:

In August 1796, six months before his death, Horace Walpole wrote a memorandum requesting his executors to "cord up strongly and seal" a large chest containing his memoirs, a vast, unpublished manuscript of some three million words. The box was to be opened only by the "first son of Lady Waldegrave who shall attain the age of twenty-five years," the key to be guarded by Lady Waldegrave herself. This oblique form of publication—a key to a box containing manuscripts in search of an editor—is emblematic of Walpole's authorial career. His most famous work, *The Castle of Otranto*, was first published spuriously as a translation from the Italian of "Onuphrio Muralto." His other principal imaginative writings, *The Mysterious Mother* and *Hieroglyphic Tales*, were issued only to a few close friends in private editions at Strawberry Hill. Walpole arranged for his collected works to be published only after his death; his collected cor-respondence has taken until 1983 to reach complete publication in the forty-eight volumes of the Yale Edition; while the memoirs, duly recovered from the sealed chest, were mangled by incompetent nineteenth-century editors and have not yet been published in full.[5]

He had a diabolical (and at times rather infantile) sense of humor, demonstrated in his passing off *The Castle of Otranto* as a translation from the Italian and in the evil comedy of one of the *Hieroglyphic Tales*, "The Peach in Brandy." He once faked a letter to Jean-Jacques Rousseau that purported to be from the King of Prussia, precipitating a heated public dispute in which Rousseau, Jacob Grimm, and others participated.

He is supposed to have composed "The Peach in Brandy," in which an archbishop accidentally swallows a human fetus, for a young girl of his acquaintance: "The preference exhibited by Walpole in his old age for the society of ladies had its corollary in his life-long preference for little girls over little boys," Dorothy Stuart assures us. "He was always a courteous knight to virgins of five; and for the delectation of one of them, Lady Anne Fitzpatrick, he wrote in 1771 the fable of the *Peach in Brandy*. This fable formed one of a series of five *Hieroglyphic Tales*.... The whimsicality of these tales," she adds uncertainly, "is such that the intended parable or satire sometimes becomes a little difficult of detection."[6] It is indeed hard to imagine the effect of this story on its original intended audience.

We may wonder too about the reaction of Lord Ossory, to whom Walpole sent a copy of the story on the occasion of Lady Ossory's miscarriage of twin sons.

In this context Kenneth Gross notes that "Walpole's tales start to take on the qualities of a nightmare."[7]

Besides *The Castle of Otranto*, the other major literary work Walpole published during his lifetime was his tragedy in blank (at first I inadvertently wrote *black*) verse, *The Mysterious Mother*. Byron admired it, calling it "a tragedy of the highest order, and not a puling love-play." It concerns a young man who, through a series of mistaken identities and unfortunate misunderstandings (no fault of his own), ends up marrying the daughter he has fathered by his mother (a bewildering set of relationships outdoing Bill Wyman). Dorothy Stuart, always charmingly sympathetic to Walpole, remarks, "It is, indeed, a little curious that his imagination—though in *The Castle of Otranto* he had toyed with the theme of incest—should have been allured by a story so sombre and so revolting."[8] In a contemporaneous review (1797), William Taylor rhapsodized that the play "has attained an excellence nearly unimpeachable" and that it "may fitly be compared with the Oedipus Tyrannus of Sophocles." Few modern readers would value it quite so highly.

Walpole was blamed by his contemporaries for the suicide of the poet Thomas Chatterton, who wrote a bitter poem addressed to Walpole before perishing in romantic despair (he drank arsenic). Walpole had concluded that the claims of the youth (Chatterton was sixteen when he wrote to him) to have discovered a collection of medieval poems by a certain "Rowley" were fraudulent. Ironically, this was, as Chatterton insinuates in his poem, just the sort of deceit one might have expected from Walpole himself:

> Walpole! I thought not I should ever see
> So mean a Heart as thine has proved to be:
> Thou, who in Luxury nurs'd behold'st with Scorn
> The boy, who Friendless, Penniless, Forlorn,
> Asks thy high Favour,—thou mayst call me Cheat—

Say, didst thou ne'er indulge in such Deceit?

Who wrote *Otranto*? But I will not chide,

Scorn I will repay with Scorn, and Pride with Pride.

Still, Walpole, still, thy Prosy Chapters write,

And twaddling letters to some Fair indite,

Laud all above thee,—Fawn and Cringe to those

Who, for thy Fame, were better Friends than Foes

Still spurn the incautious Fool who dares —— ——

Had I the Gifts of Wealth and Lux'ry shar'd

Not poor and Mean—Walpole! thou hadst not dared

Thus to insult, But I shall live and Stand

By Rowley's side—when Thou art dead and damned.

✦ ✦ ✦

The Castle of Otranto is the work by which most people know Walpole (it has been published in more than a hundred and fifty editions), because of its historical significance as the first Gothic novel. It is hard now to appreciate how innovative a book this was, since countless other works have been patterned after it. Walter Scott admired the book, praising its "pure and correct English" as well as its status as "the first modern attempt to found a tale of amusing fiction upon the basis of the ancient romances of chivalry." In contrast, the writer of Walpole's obituary in *Gentlemen's Magazine* (1797), though finding much to praise in Walpole's writings, flatly dismissed *The Castle of Otranto* as "miserable trash." The book had its genesis in a dream in which Walpole found himself in an ancient castle, facing an enormous hand encased in armor. The novel is filled with ghosts, giants, mysterious appearances, and violent emotions. "I gave rein to my imagination," Walpole said, "Visions and passions choked me." In this classic work Walpole began to develop his taste for the Gothic and the grotesque and, more fundamentally, to tap the turbulent world of his unconscious in a manner shocking for his time, to take us closer to the terrifying psychological substrata that have become a major literary subject in our own century. Nonetheless, *The Castle* remains a rather mechanical and distanced work. It was not until the *Hieroglyphic Tales* that Walpole began to discover a more radical way of writing that anticipated a direction taken in modern fiction.

Walpole wrote in his postscript to the *Hieroglyphic Tales* that the tales were an attempt "to vary the stale and beaten class of stories and novels, which, though works of invention, are almost always devoid of imagination. It would scarcely be credited, were it not evident from the Bibliotheque des Romans, which contains the fictitious adventures that have been written in all ages and all countries, that there should have been so little fancy, so little variety, and so little novelty, in writings in which the imagination is fettered by no rules, and by no obligation of speaking truth. There is infinitely more invention in history, which has no merit if devoid of truth, than in romances and novels, which pretend to none."

This is an attitude with which many editors and publishers will sympathize, for we know that fiction manuscripts are distinguished more than anything else by their striking similarity to one another. How hard it is to be truly imaginative! In the *Hieroglyphic Tales* Walpole worked out a number of ways of breaking from the mold.

First, he structured his stories on a firm "fairy tale" foundation. Kenneth Gross calls the tales representatives of a tradition of "oriental fables" that also found expression in such works of the period as Voltaire's *Zadig*, Crébillon's *Le Sopha*, and Johnson's *Rasselas*. "Judged for themselves, however," he adds, "the tales are a small miracle. The best of them distill from the Bible, the Arabian Nights, Shakespeare, French romances, English politics, and antiquarian lore a comic fantasy of an urbane, hard-edged strangeness such as it is hard to find anywhere else...."[9]

The familiarity of this form enabled Walpole to make bold innovations in other aspects of his narrative. "Music rots when it gets *too far* from the dance," Ezra Pound admonished in *ABC of Reading*, and "poetry atrophies when it gets too far from music." By the same token, narrative fiction atrophies when it gets too far from the foundations of storytelling: myths and folktales. Walpole was wise to graft his grotesque elaborations on a sturdy folktale rootstock.

(We might add that typography atrophies when it gets too far from handwriting. This book is set in a version of the typeface designed by and named for the eighteenth-century English typographer William Caslon. It is the last of the original Old Style typefaces derived from the Renaissance scribal tradition, and it is the face in which Walpole set his first edition of the *Hieroglyphic Tales*.)

Among the most innovative of Walpole's narrative effects was his radical subversion of the representational fallacy. He strewed impossibilities through the stories (*choses absurdes et hors de toute vraisemblance*, as the epigraph has it), leaving the reader to puzzle over the ability of narrative

and of language itself to confound our understanding of the relation between language, storytelling, and reality. The tales are opaque, calling as
much attention to the telling as to the stories themselves. They were written, he tells us in the preface, compounding impossibilities one upon
another, "a little before the creation of the world, and have ever since been
preserved, by oral tradition, in the mountains of Crampcraggiri, an uninhabited island, not yet discovered." He peopled the stories with dead
suitors, daughters who were never born (or, being born, are proven not to
exist), and such fancies as goats' eggs sought as a cure for freckles.

In addition, Walpole disrupted the narrative continuity of his stories
with detours, denials, false starts, solipsisms, and asides. In part this probably derived from a private symbolism in which characters and incidents
cloaked catty personal allusions to political or society figures, allusions now
largely lost; but the result was a narrative that delights and perplexes with
its off-center unpredictability. Walpole created an existential narrative,

remarkable for its age, existing simply to be and not to refer. Kenneth Gross crafts a subtle paragraph on this theme:

> A constitutive intellectual drama underlies the most outlandish projects of Swift's imperturbable madmen, such as the idea of finding capable politicians, preachers, and journalists in the lower reaches of Bedlam. But Walpole's brief narratives tend to liberate the fantasies of satire from the bondage of ideas. That is to say, his tales make use of the exaggerated, ironic fictions of satire as much as the more self-consistent magical devices of fairy tales, but their bizarre, mannerist surfaces seem continually to deny the possibility of a concealed intellectual skeleton. Despite a wealth of literary and historical allusion, and many *moments* of sharp, ironic criticism, Walpole's hieroglyphics do not in-vite us to read them as ciphers of an integrated satiric argument.[10]

In one modern vocabulary we might say that Walpole, surprisingly for such a seemingly intellectual, cynical, satiric character, somehow transcended his own gravest limitations to succeed as much as any writer of his time in freeing the story from the restraints of the ego (while maintaining a profoundly ambivalent attitude to the whole undertaking).

Finally, Walpole played with tone in an extremely innovative and sophisticated way. His habitual skepticism played against the fairy-tale suspension of disbelief and his own wild flights of fancy (thus he began *Hieroglyphic Tales* with an inverted Scheherazade story — "whose own tales might be said to represent the power of fantastic narrative at its purest" — in which the captive princess bores her husband to sleep and then kills him.)[11] Likewise, his wicked, at times unpleasant wit played against the faux naïveté of the fairy-tale narrative to create an unusually rich style, full of color and texture.

✦ ✦ ✦

Walpole, as we have seen, was as a rule skittish about publication; this was particularly true of the Hieroglyphic Tales. Perhaps this was due in part to a rumor that he was in possession of tales of an unprecedented strangeness, which he had written in the throes of delirium. "I have some strange things in my drawer, even wilder than The Castle of Otranto," he allowed in a letter to the Reverend William Cole in 1779, "but they were not written lately [the *Tales* were composed between 1766 and 1772], nor in the gout, nor, whatever they may seem, written while I was out of my senses."[12] Six years later he printed six or seven (counting a proof printing) copies, all of which he kept in his own possession until his death. Until the twentieth century, this was the only publication of this extraordinary work.[13] (Tongue in cheek, Walpole estimated that "it will be treated with due reverence some hundred ages hence.") In 1926 a small limited edition was published in England by Elkin Matthews. In 1982 another small edition (a facsimile of the original 1785 printing) was published by the Augustan Reprint Society of the University of California, Los Angeles. This edition included a helpful introduction by Kenneth Gross (from which I have quoted), and to it was appended an additional tale, "The Bird's Nest," first brought to light by A. Dayle Wallace, which had once been intended by Walpole for the collection but was not included in his original printing.[14]

This Mercury House edition is thus the first publication ever for the general trade of this strange, innovative, singular work, still funny and still disturbing—and still particularly provocative to anyone interested in the art of storytelling—after more than two centuries. We have included "The Bird's Nest," and we have followed Walpole's somewhat eccentric spelling, punctuation, and styling but have replaced the eighteenth-century long esses of the Strawberry Hill printing with modern ones. We are pleased to present the *Hieroglyphic Tales* in a handsome paperback edition with a second interior color and beautiful, witty illustrations, remarkably sensitive to the tone and spirit of the text, by Jill McElmurry of Dunsmuir, California.

Altogether a suitable edition for your Walpolling activities.

— *Thomas Christensen*

NOTES

1. Diane S. Ames, "Strawberry Hill: Architecture of the 'as if,' " in *Studies in Eighteenth-Century Culture 8*, ed. Roseann Runte (Madison: University of Wisconsin Press, 1979), cited in Peter Sabor, *Horace Walpole: A Reference Guide* (Boston: G. K. Hall & Co., 1984), 230.

2. "Strawberry Hill," *Builder* 41 (August 13, 1881), cited in Sabor, 76.

3. Douglas McMurtrie, *The Book: The Story of Printing and Bookmaking* (London: Oxford University Press, 1943), 464.

4. Daniel Berkeley Updike, *Printing Types: Their History, Forms, and Use,* vol. 2 (1937; reprint, New York: Dover Publications, 1980), 140.

5. Sabor, 1.

6. Dorothy Margaret Stuart, *Horace Walpole* (New York: Macmillan, 1927), 191.

7. Kenneth W. Gross, in *Hieroglyphic Tales,* Horace Walpole (Los Angeles: University of California Augustan Reprint Society, 1982), x.

8. Stuart, 181.

9. Gross, iii.

10. Gross, v.

11. Gross, ix.

12. Gross, iii.

13. I have encountered a reference to an 1822 edition but have not been able to verify it. No such edition is listed in Peter Sabor's comprehensive *Horace Walpole: A Reference Guide* (Boston: G. K. Hall & Co., 1984), which asserts that the 1926 edition was the first since the original printing.

14. A. Dayle Wallace, "Two Unpublished Fairy Tales by Horace Walpole," in *Horace Walpole: Writer, Politician, and Connoisseur,* ed. Warren Hunting Smith (New Haven: Yale University Press, 1967), 241–53.

Hieroglyphic Tales

Schah Baham ne comprenoit jamais bien que les choses absurdes & hors de toute vraisemblance.

Le Sopha, p. 5.

Preface

As the invaluable present I am making to the world may not please all tastes, from the gravity of the matter, the solidity of the reasoning, and the deep learning contained in the ensuing sheets, it is necessary to make some apology for producing this work in so trifling an age, when nothing will go down but temporary politics, personal satire, and idle romances. The true reason then for my surmounting all these objections was singly this: I was apprehensive lest the work should be lost to posterity; and though it may be condemned at present, I can have no doubt but it will be treated with due reverence some hundred ages hence, when wisdom and learning shall have gained their proper ascendant over mankind, and when men shall only read for instruction and improvement of their minds. As I shall print an hundred thousand copies some, it may be hoped, will escape the havoc that is made of moral works, and then this jewel will shine forth in its genuine lustre. I was in the greater hurry to consign this work to the press, as I foresee that the art of printing will ere long be totally lost, like other useful discoveries well known to the ancients. Such were the art of dissolving rocks with hot vinegar, of teaching elephants to dance on the slack rope, of making malleable glass, of writing epic poems that any body would read after they had been published a month, and the stupendous invention of new religions, a secret of which illiterate Mahomet was the last person possessed.

Notwithstanding this my zeal for good letters, and the ardour of my universal citizenship, (for I declare I design this present for all nations) there are some small difficulties in the way, that prevent my conferring this my great benefaction on the world compleatly and all at once. I am obliged to produce it in small portions, and therefore beg the prayers of all good and wise men that my life may be prolonged to me, till I shall be able to publish the whole work, no man else being capable of executing the charge so well as myself, for reasons that my modesty will not permit me to specify. In the mean time, as it is the duty of an editor to acquaint the world with what relates to himself as well as his author, I think it right to mention the causes that compel me to publish this work in numbers. The common reason of such proceeding is to make a book dearer for the ease of the purchasers, it being supposed that most people had rather give twenty shillings by six-pence a fortnight, than pay ten shillings once for all. Public spirited as this proceeding is, I must confess my reasons are more and merely personal. As my circumstances are very moderate, and barely sufficient to maintain decently a gentleman of my abilities and learning, I cannot afford to print at once an hundred thousand copies of two volumes in folio, for that will be the whole mass of Hieroglyphic Tales when the work is perfected. In the next place, being very asthmatic, and requiring a free communication of air, I lodge in the uppermost story of a house in an alley not far from St. Mary Axe; and as a great deal of good company lodges in the same mansion, it was by a considerable favour that I could obtain a single chamber to myself; which chamber is by no means large enough to contain the whole impression, for I design to vend the copies myself, and, according to the practice of other great men, shall sign the first sheet myself with my own hand.

Desirous as I am of acquainting the world with many more circumstances relative to myself, some private considerations prevent my indulging their curiosity any farther at present; but I shall take care to leave so minute an account of myself to some public library, that the future commentators and editors of this work shall not be deprived of all necessary lights. In the mean time I beg the reader to accept the temporary compensation of an account of the author whose work I am publishing.

The Hieroglyphic Tales were undoubtedly written a little before the creation of the world, and have ever since been preserved, by oral tradition, in the mountains of Crampcraggiri, an uninhabited island, not yet discovered. Of these few facts we could have the most authentic attestations of several clergymen, who remember to have heard them repeated by old men long before they, the said clergymen, were born. We do not trouble the reader with these attestations, as we are sure every body will believe them as much as if they had seen them. It is more difficult to ascertain the true author. We might ascribe them with great probability to Kemanrlegorpikos, son of Quat; but besides that we are not certain that any such person ever existed, it is not clear that he ever wrote any thing but a book of cookery, and that in heroic verse. Others give them to Quat's nurse, and a few to Hermes Trismegistus, though there is a passage in the latter's treatise on the harpsichord which directly contradicts the account of the first volcano in the 114th of the Hieroglyphic Tales. As Trismegistus's work is lost, it is impossible to decide now whether the discordance mentioned is so positive as has been asserted by many learned men, who only guess at the opinion of Hermes from other passages in his writings, and who indeed are not sure whether he was speaking of volcanoes or cheesecakes, for he drew so ill, that his hieroglyphics may often be taken for the most opposite things in nature; and as there is no subject which he has not treated, it is not precisely known what he was discussing in any one of them.

This is the nearest we can come to any certainty with regard to the author. But whether he wrote the Tales six thousand years ago, as we believe, or whether they were written for him within these ten years, they are incontestably the most ancient work in the world; and though there is little imagination, and still less invention in them; yet there are so many passages in them exactly resembling Homer, that any man living would conclude they were imitated from that great poet, if it was not certain that Homer borrowed from them, which I shall prove two ways: first, by giving Homer's parallel passages at the bottom of the page; and secondly, by translating Homer himself into prose, which shall make him so unlike himself, that nobody will think he could be an original writer: and when he is become totally lifeless and insipid, it will be impossible but these Tales should be preferred to the Iliad; especially as I design to put them into a kind of style that shall be neither verse nor prose; a diction lately much used in tragedies and heroic poems, the former of which are really heroic poems from want of probability, as an antico-moderno epic poem is in fact a meer tragedy, having little or no change of scene, no incidents but a ghost and a storm, and no events but the deaths of the principal actors.

I will not detain the reader longer from the perusal of this invaluable work; but I must beseech the public to be expeditious in taking off the whole impression, as fast as I can get it printed; because I must inform them that I have a more precious work in contemplation; namely, a new Roman history, in which I mean to ridicule, detect and expose, all ancient virtue, and patriotism, and shew from original papers which I am going to write, and which I shall afterwards bury in the ruins of Carthage and then dig up, that it appears by the letters of Hanno the Punic embassador at Rome, that Scipio was in the pay of Hannibal, and that the dilatoriness of Fabius proceeded from his being a pensioner of the same general. I own this discovery will pierce my heart; but as morality is best taught by shewing how little effect it had on the best of men, I will sacrifice the most virtuous names for the instruction of the present wicked generation; and I cannot doubt but when once they have learnt to detest the favourite heroes of antiquity, they will become good subjects of the most pious king that ever lived since David, who expelled the established royal family, and then sung psalms to the memory of Jonathan, to whose prejudice he had succeeded to the throne.

A New Arabian Night's Entertainment

Tale I

At the foot of the great mountain Hirgonqúu was anciently situated the kingdom of Larbidel. Geographers, who are not apt to make such just comparisons, said, it resembled a football just going to be kicked away; and so it happened; for the mountain kicked the kingdom into the ocean, and it has never been heard of since.

One day a young princess had climbed up to the top of the mountain to gather goat's eggs, the whites of which are excellent for taking off freckles.—Goat's eggs!—Yes—naturalists hold that all Beings are conceived in an egg. The goats of Hirgonqúu might be oviparous, and lay their eggs to be hatched by the sun. This is my supposition; no matter whether I believe it myself or not. I will write against and abuse any man that opposes my hypothesis. It would be fine indeed if learned men were obliged to believe what they assert.

The other side of the mountain was inhabited by a nation of whom the Larbidellians knew no more than the French nobility do of Great Britain, which they think is an island that some how or other may be approached by land. The princess had strayed into the confines of Cucurucu, when she suddenly found herself seized by the guards of the prince that reigned in that country. They told her in few words that she must be conveyed to the capital and married to the giant their lord and emperor. The giant, it seems, was fond of having a new wife every night, who was to tell him a story that would last till morning, and then have her head cut off—such odd ways have some folks of passing their wedding nights! The princess modestly asked, why their master loved such long stories? The captain of the guard replied, his majesty did not sleep well—Well! said she, and if he does not!—not but I believe I can tell as long stories as any princess in Asia. Nay, I can repeat Leonidas by Heart, and your emperor must be wakeful indeed if he can hold out against that.

By this time they were arrived at the palace. To the great surprise of the princess, the emperor, so far from being a giant, was but five feet one inch in height; but being two inches taller than any of his predecessors, the flattery of his courtiers had bestowed the name of *giant* on him; and he affected to look down upon any man above his own stature. The princess was immediately undressed and put to bed, his majesty being impatient to hear a new story.

Light of my eyes, said the emperor, what is your name? I call myself the princess of Gronovia, replied she; but my real appellation is the frow Gronow. And what is the use of a name, said his majesty, but to be called by it? And why do you pretend to be a princess, if you are not? My turn is romantic, answered she, and I have ever had an ambition of being the heroine of a novel. Now there are but two conditions that entitle one to that rank; one must be a shepherdess or a princess. Well, content yourself, said the giant, you will die an empress, without being either the one or the other! But what sublime reason had you for lengthening your name so unaccountably? It is a custom in my family, said she: all my ancestors were learned men, who wrote about the Romans. It sounded more classic, and gave a higher opinion of their literature, to put a Latin termination to

their names. All this is Japonese to me, said the emperor; but your ancestors seem to have been a parcel of mountebanks. Does one understand any
thing the better for corrupting one's name? Oh, said the princess, but it
shewed taste too. There was a time when in Italy the learned carried this
still farther; and a man with a large forehead, who was born on the fifth on
January, called himself Quintus Januarius Fronto. More and more absurd,
said the emperor. You seem to have a great deal of impertinent knowledge
about a great many impertinent people; but proceed in your story: whence
came you? Mynheer, said she, I was born in Holland—The deuce you
was, said the emperor, and where is that? It was no where, replied the
princess, spritelily, till my countrymen gained it from the sea—Indeed,
moppet! said his majesty; and pray who were your countrymen, before you
had any country? Your majesty asks a vey shrewd question, said she, which
I cannot resolve on a sudden; but I will step home to my library, and con-
sult five or six thousand volumes of modern history, an hundred or two

dictionaries, and an abridgement of geography in forty volumes in folio, and be back in an instant. Not so fast, my life, said the emperor, you must not rise till you go to execution; it is now one in the morning, and you have not begun your story.

My great grandfather, continued the princess, was a Dutch merchant, who passed many years in Japan—On what account? said the emperor. He went thither to abjure his religion, said she, that he might get money enough to return and defend it against Philip 2^d. You are a pleasant family, said the emperor; but though I love fables, I hate genealogies. I know in all families, by their own account, there never was any thing but good and great men from father to son; a sort of fiction that does not at all amuse me. In my dominions there is no nobility but flattery. Whoever flatters me best is created a great lord, and the titles I confer are synonimous to their merits. There is Kiss-my-breech-Can, my favourite; Adulation-Can, lord treasurer; Prerogative-Can, head of the law; and Blasphemy-Can, high-priest. Whoever speaks truth, corrupts his blood, and is ipso facto degraded. In Europe you allow a man to be noble because one of his ancestors was a flatterer. But every thing degenerates, the farther it is removed from its source. I will not hear a word of any of your race before your father: what was he?

It was in the height of the contests about the bull unigenitus—I tell you, interrupted the emperor, I will not be plagued with any more of those people with Latin names: they were a parcel of coxcombs, and seem to have infected you with their folly. I am sorry, replied Gronovia, that your sublime highness is so little acquainted with the state of Europe, as to take a papal ordinance for a person. Unigenitus is Latin for the Jesuits—And who the devil are the Jesuits? said the giant. You explain one nonsensical term by another, and wonder I am never the wiser. Sir, said the princess, if you will permit me to give you a short account of the troubles that have agitated Europe for these last two hundred years, on the doctrines of grace, free-will, predestination, reprobation, justification, &c. you will be more entertained, and will believe less, than if I told your majesty a long tale of fairies and goblins. You are an eternal prater, said the emperor, and very self-sufficient; but talk your fill, and upon what subject you like, till tomorrow morning; but I swear by the soul of the holy Jirigi, who rode to heaven on the tail of a magpie, as soon as the clock strikes eight, you are a dead woman. Well, who was the Jesuit Unigenitus?

The novel doctrines that had sprung up in Germany, said Gronovia, made it necessary for the church to look about her. The disciples of Loyola—Of whom? said the emperor, yawning—Ignatius Loyola, the founder of the Jesuits, replied Gronovia, was—A writer of Roman history, I suppose, interrupted the emperor: what the devil were the Romans to you, that you trouble your head so much about them? The empire of Rome, and the church of Rome, are two distinct things, said the princess; and yet, as one may say, the one depends upon the other, as the new testament does on the old. One destroyed the other, and yet pretends a right to its inheritance. The temporalities of the church—What's o'clock, said the emperor to the chief eunuch? it cannot sure be far from eight—this woman has gossipped at least seven hours. Do you hear, my tomorrow-night's wife shall be dumb—cut her tongue out before you bring her to our bed. Madam, said the eunuch, his sublime highness, whose erudition passes the sands of the sea, is too well acquainted with all human sciences to require information. It is therefore that his exalted wisdom prefers accounts of what never happened, to any relation either in history or divinity—You lie, said the emperor; when I exclude truth, I certainly do not mean to forbid divinity—How many divinities have you in Europe, woman? The council of Trent, replied Gronovia, has decided—the emperor began to snore—I mean, continued Gronovia, that notwithstanding all father Paul has asserted, cardinal Palavicini affirms that in the three first sessions of that council—the emperor was now fast asleep, which the princess and the chief eunuch perceiving, clapped several pillows upon his face, and held them there till he expired. As soon as they were convinced he was dead, the princess, putting on every mark of despair and concern, issued to the divan, where she was immediately proclaimed empress. The emperor, it was given out, had died of an hermorrhoidal cholic, but to shew her regard for his memory, her imperial majesty declared she would strictly adhere to the maxims by which he had governed. Accordingly she espoused a new husband every night, but dispensed with their telling her stories, and was graciously pleased also, upon their good behaviour, to remit the subsequent execution. She sent presents to all the learned men in Asia; and they in return did not fail to cry her up as a pattern of clemency, wisdom, and virtue: and though the panegyrics of the learned are generally as clumsy as they are fulsome, they ventured to assure her that their writings would be as durable as brass, and that the memory of her glorious reign would reach to the latest posterity.

The King and His Three Daughters

Tale II

There was formerly a king, who had three daughters—that is, he would have had three, if he had had one more, but some how or other the eldest never was born. She was extremely handsome, had a great deal of wit, and spoke French in perfection, as all the authors of that age affirm, and yet none of them pretend that she ever existed. It is very certain that the two other princesses were far from beauties; the second had a strong Yorkshire dialect, and the youngest had bad teeth and but one leg, which occasioned her dancing very ill.

As it was not probable that his majesty would have any more children, being eighty-seven years, two months, and thirteen days old when his queen died, the states of the kingdom were very anxious to have the princesses married. But there was one great obstacle to this settlement, though so important to the peace of the kingdom. The king insisted that his eldest daughter should be married first, and as there was no such person, it was very difficult to fix upon a proper husband for her. The courtiers all approved his majesty's resolution; but as under the best princes there will always be a number of discontented, the nation was torn into different factions, the grumblers or patriots insisting that the second princess was the eldest, and ought to be declared heiress apparent to the crown. Many pamphlets were written pro and con, but the ministerial party pretended that the chancellor's argument was unanswerable, who affirmed, that the second princess could not be the eldest, as no princess-royal ever had a Yorkshire accent. A few persons who were attached to the youngest princess, took advantage of this plea for whispering that *her* royal highness's pretensions to the crown were the best of all; for as there was no eldest princess, and as the second must be the first, if there was no first, and as she could not be the second if she was the first, and as the chancellor had proved that she could not be the first, it followed plainly by every idea of law that she could be nobody at all; and then the consequence followed of course, that the youngest must be the eldest, if she had no elder sister.

It is inconceivable what animosities and mischiefs arose from these different titles; and each faction endeavoured to strengthen itself by foreign alliances. The court party having no real object for their attachment, were the most attached of all, and made up by warmth for the want of foundation in their principles. The clergy in general were devoted to this, which was styled *the first party*. The physicians embraced the second; and the lawyers declared for the third, or the faction of the youngest princess, because it seemed best calculated to admit of doubts and endless litigation.

While the nation was in this distracted situation, there arrived the prince of Quifferiquimini, who would have been the most accomplished hero of the age, if he had not been dead, and had spoken any language but the Egyptian, and had not had three legs. Notwithstanding these blemishes, the eyes of the whole nation were immediately turned upon him, and each party wished to see him married to the princess whose cause they espoused.

The old king received him with the most distinguished honours; the senate made the most fulsome addresses to him; the princesses were so taken with him, that they grew more bitter enemies than ever; and the court ladies and petit-maitres invented a thousand new fashions upon his account—every thing was to be à la Quifferiquimini. Both men and women of fashion left off rouge to look the more cadaverous; their cloaths were embroidered with hieroglyphics, and all the ugly characters they could gather from Egyptian antiquities, with which they were forced to be contented, it being impossible to learn a language that is lost; and all tables, chairs, stools, cabinets and couches, were made with only three legs; the last, however, soon went out of fashion, as being very inconvenient.

The prince, who, ever since his death, had had but a weakly constitution, was a little fatigued with this excess of attentions, and would often wish himself at home in his coffin. But his greatest difficulty of all was to get rid of the youngest princess, who kept hopping after him wherever he went, and was so full of admiration of his three legs, and so modest about having but one herself, and so inquisitive to know how his three legs were set on, that being the best natured man in the world, it went to his heart whenever in a fit of peevishness he happened to drop an impatient word, which never failed to throw her into an agony of tears, and then she looked so ugly that it was impossible for him to be tolerably civil to her. He was not much more inclined to the second princess—In truth, it was the eldest who made the conquest of his affections: and so violently did his passion encrease one Tuesday morning, that breaking through all prudential considerations (for there were many reasons which ought to have determined his choice in favour of either of the other sisters) he hurried to the old king, acquainted him with his love, and demanded the eldest princess in marriage. Nothing could equal the joy of the good old monarch, who wished for nothing but to live to see the consummation of this match. Throwing his arms about the prince-skeleton's neck and watering his hollow cheeks with warm tears, he granted his request, and added, that he would immediately resign his crown to him and his favourite daughter.

I am forced for want of room to pass over many circumstances that would add greatly to the beauty of this history, and am sorry I must dash the reader's impatience by acquainting him, that notwithstanding the eagerness of the old king and youthful ardour of the prince, the nuptials were obliged to be postponed; the archbishop declaring that it was essentially necessary to have a dispensation from the pope, the parties being related within the forbidden degrees; a woman that never was, and a man that had been, being deemed first cousins in the eye of the canon law.

Hence arose a new difficulty. The religion of the Quifferiquiminians was totally opposite to that of the papists. The former believed in nothing but grace; and they had a high-priest of their own, who pretended that he was master of the whole fee-simple of grace, and by that possession could cause every thing to have been that never had been, and could prevent every thing that had been from ever having been. "We have nothing to do, said the prince to the king, but to send a solemn embassy to the high-priest of grace, with a present of a hundred thousand million of ingots, and he will cause your charming no-daughter to have been, and will prevent my having died, and then there will be no occasion for a dispensation from your old fool at Rome."—How! thou impious, atheistical bag of drybones, cried the old king; dost thou profane our holy religion? Thou shalt have no daughter of mine, thou three-legged skeleton—Go and be buried and be damned, as thou must be; for as thou art dead, thou art past repentance: I would sooner give my child to a baboon, who has one leg more than thou hast, than bestow her on such a reprobate corpse—You had better give your one-legged infanta to the baboon, said the prince, they are fitter for one another—As much a corpse as I am, I am preferable to nobody; and who the devil would have married your no-daughter, but a dead body! For my religion, I lived and died in it, and it is not in my power to change it now if I would—but for your part—a great shout interrupted this dialogue, and the captain of the guard rushing into the royal closet, acquainted his majesty, that the second princess, in revenge of the prince's neglect, had given her hand to a drysalter, who was a common-council man, and that the city, in consideration of the match, had proclaimed them king and queen, allowing his majesty to retain the title for his life, which they had fixed for the term of six months; and ordering, in respect of his royal birth, that the prince should immediately lie in state and have a pompous funeral.

This revolution was so sudden and so universal, that all parties approved, or were forced to seem to approve it. The old king died the next day, as the courtiers said, for joy; the prince of Quifferiquimini was buried in spite of his appeal to the law of nations; and the youngest princess went distracted, and was shut up in a madhouse, calling out day and night for a husband with three legs.

The Dice-Box.
A Fairy Tale
Tale III

*Translated from the French Translation of the
Countess DAUNOIS, for the Entertainment of
Miss CAROLINE CAMPBELL.

T here was a merchant of Damascus named Aboulcasem,

who had an only daughter called Pissimissi, which signi-

fies *the waters of Jordan*; because a fairy foretold at her

birth that she would be one of Solomon's concubines. Azaziel, the angel of

---

*Eldest daughter of lord William Campbell; she lived with her aunt the countess of Ailesbury.

35

death, having transported Aboulcasem to the regions of bliss, he had no fortune to bequeath to his beloved child but the shell of a pistachia-nut drawn by an elephant and a ladybird. Pissimissi, who was but nine years old, and who had been kept in great confinement, was impatient to see the world; and no sooner was the breath out of her father's body, than she got into the car, and whipping her elephant and ladybird, drove out of the yard as fast as possible, without knowing whither she was going. Her coursers never stopped till they came to the foot of a brazen tower, that had neither doors nor windows, in which lived an old enchantress, who had locked herself up there with seventeen thousand husbands. It had but one single vent for air, which was a small chimney grated over, through which it was scarce possible to put one's hand. Pissimissi, who was very impatient, ordered her coursers to fly with her up to the top of the chimney, which, as they were the most docile creatures in the world, they immediately did; but unluckily the fore paw of the elephant lighting on the top of the chimney, broke down the grate by its weight, but at the same time stopped up the passage so entirely, that all the enchantress's husbands were stifled for want of air. As it was a collection she had made with great care and cost, it is easy to imagine her vexation and rage. She raised a storm of thunder and lightning that lasted eight hundred and four years; and having conjured up an army of two thousand devils, she ordered them to flay the elephant alive, and dress it for her supper with anchovy sauce. Nothing could have saved the poor beast, if, struggling to get loose from the chimney, he had not happily broken wind, which it seems is a great preservative against devils. They all flew a thousand ways, and in their hurry carried away half the brazen tower, by which means the elephant, the car, the ladybird, and Pissimissi got loose; but in their fall tumbled through the roof of an apothecary's shop, and broke all his bottles of physic. The elephant, who was very dry with his fatigue, and who had not much taste, immediately sucked up all the medicines with his proboscis, which occasioned such a variety of effects in his bowels, that it was well he had such a strong constitution, or he must have died of it. His evacuations were so plentiful, that he not only drowned the tower of Babel, near which the apothecary's shop stood, but the current ran fourscore leagues till it came to the sea, and there poisoned so many whales and leviathans, that a pestilence ensued, and lasted three years, nine months and sixteen days. As the elephant was extremely weakened by what had happened, it was impossible for him to draw the car for eighteen months, which was a cruel delay to Pissimissi's impatience, who during all that time could not travel above a hundred miles a day, for as she carried the sick animal in her lap, the poor ladybird could not make longer stages with no assistance. Besides, Pissimissi bought every thing she saw wherever she came; and all was crouded into the car and stuffed into the seat. She had purchased ninety-two dolls, seventeen baby-houses, six cart-loads of sugar-plumbs, a thousand ells of gingerbread, eight dancing dogs, a bear and a monkey, four toy-shops with all their contents, and seven dozen of bibs and aprons of the newest fashion. They were jogging on with all this cargo over mount Caucasus, when an immense humming-bird, who had been struck with the beauty of the ladybird's wings, that I had forgot to say were of ruby spotted with black pearls, sousing down at once on her prey, swallowed ladybird, Pissimissi, the elephant, and all their commodities. It happened that the humming-bird belonged to Solomon; he let it out of its cage every morning after breakfast, and it constantly came home by the time the council broke up. Nothing could equal the surprise of his majesty and the courtiers, when the dear little creature arrived with the elephant's proboscis hanging out of its divine little bill. However, after the first astonishment was over, his majesty, who to be sure was wisdom itself, and who understood natural philosophy that it was a charm to hear him discourse of those matters, and who was actually making a collection of dried beasts and birds in twelve thousand volumes of the best fool's-cap paper, immediately perceived what

had happened, and taking out of the side pocket of his breeches a dia-
mond toothpick-case of his own turning, with the toothpick made of the
only unicorn's horn he ever saw, he stuck it into the elephant's snout, and
began to draw it out: but all his philosophy was confounded, when
jammed between the elephant's legs he perceived the head of a beautiful
girl, and between her legs a baby-house, which with the wings extended
thirty feet, out of the windows of which rained a torrent of sugar-plumbs,
that had been placed there to make room. Then followed the bear, who
had been pressed to the bales of gingerbread and was covered all over with
it, and looked but uncouthly; and the monkey with a doll in every paw,
and his pouches so crammed with sugar-plumbs that they hung on each
side of him, and trailed on the ground behind like the duchess of ********'s
beautiful breasts. Solomon, however, gave small attention to this proces-
sion, being caught with the charms of the lovely Pissimissi: he immediately
began the song of songs extempore; and what he had seen—I mean, all

that came out of the humming-bird's throat had made such a jumble in his ideas, that there was nothing so unlike to which he did not compare all Pissimissi's beauties. As he sung his canticles too to no tune, and god knows had but a bad voice, they were far from comforting Pissimissi: the elephant had torn her best bib and apron, and she cried and roared, and kept such a squalling, that though Solomon carried her in his arms, and showed her all the fine things in the temple, there was no pacifying her. The queen of Sheba, who was playing at backgammon with the high-priest, and who came every October to converse with Solomon, though she did not understand a word of Hebrew, hearing the noise, came running out of her dressing-room; and seeing the king with a squalling child in his arms, asked him peevishly, if it became his reputed wisdom to expose himself with his bastards to all the court? Solomon, instead of replying, kept singing, "We have a little sister, and she has no breasts;" which so provoked the Sheban princess, that happening to have one of the dice-boxes in her hand, she without any ceremony threw it at his head. The enchantress, whom I mentioned before, and who, though invisible, had followed Pissimissi, and drawn her into her train of misfortunes, turned the dice-box aside, and directed it to Pissimissi's nose, which being something flat, like madame de ********'s, it stuck there, and being of ivory, Solomon ever after compared his beloved's nose to the tower that leads to Damascus. The queen, though ashamed of her behaviour, was not in her heart sorry for the accident; but when she found that it only encreased the monarch's passion, her contempt redoubled; and calling him a thousand old fools to herself, she ordered her postchaise and drove away in a fury, without leaving sixpence for the servants; and nobody knows what became of her or her kingdom, which has never been heard of since.

The Peach
in Brandy
A Milesian Tale

Tale IV

itz Scanlan Mac Giolla l'ha druig,[1] king of Kilkenny, the thousand and fifty-seventh descendant in a direct line from Milesius king of Spain, had an only daughter called Great A, and by corruption Grata; who being arrived at years of discretion, and perfectly initiated by her royal parents in the arts of government, the fond monarch determined to resign his crown to her: having accordingly assembled the senate, he declared his resolution to them, and having delivered his sceptre into the princess's hand, he obliged her to ascend the throne; and to set the example, was the first to kiss her hand, and vow eternal obedience to her. The senators were ready to stifle the new queen with panegyrics and addresses; the people, though they adored the old king, were transported with having a new sovereign, and the university, according to custom immemorial, presented her majesty, three months after every body had forgotten the event, with testimonials of the excessive sorrow and excessive joy they felt on losing one monarch and getting another.

Her majesty was now in the fifth year of the age, and a prodigy of sense and goodness. In her first speech to the senate, which she lisped with inimitable grace, she assured them that her^2 heart was entirely Irish, and that she did not intend any longer to go in leading-strings, as a proof of which she immediately declared her nurse prime-minister. The senate applauded this sage choice with even greater encomiums than the last, and voted a free gift to the queen of a million of sugar-plumbs, and to the favourite of twenty thousand bottles of usquebaugh. Her majesty then jumping from her throne, declared it was her royal pleasure to play at blindman's buff, but such a hub-bub arose from the senators pushing, and pressing, and squeezing, and punching one another, to endeavour to be the first blinded, that in the scuffle her majesty was thrown down and got a bump on her forehead as big as a pigeon's egg, which set her a squalling, that you might have heard her to Tipperary. The old king flew into a rage, and snatching up the mace knocked out the chancellor's brains, who at that time happened not to have any; and the queen-mother, who sat in a tribune above to see the ceremony, fell into a fit and[3] miscarried of twins, who were killed by her majesty's fright; but the earl of Bullaboo, great butler of the crown, happening to stand next to the queen, catched up one of the dead children, and perceiving it was a boy, ran down to the[4] king and wished him joy of the birth of a son and heir. The king, who had now recovered his sweet temper, called him a fool and blunderer, upon which Mr. Phelim O'Torture, a zealous courtier, started up with great presence of mind and accused the earl of Bullaboo of high treason, for having asserted that his late majesty had had any other heir than their present most lawful and most religious sovereign queen Grata. An impeachment was voted by a large majority, though not without warm opposition, particularly from a celebrated Kilkennian orator, whose name is unfortunately not come down to us, it being erased out of the journals afterwards, as the Irish author whom I copy says, when he became first lord of the treasury, as he was during the whole reign of queen Grata's successor. The argument of this Mr. Killmorackill, says my author, whose name is lost, was, that her majesty the queen-mother having conceived a son before the king's resignation, that son was indubitably heir to the crown, and consequently the resignation void, it not signifying an iota whether the child was born alive or dead: it was alive, said he, when it was conceived—here he was called to order by Dr. O'Flaharty, the queen-mother's man-midwife and member for the borough of Corbelly, who entered into a learned dissertation on embrios; but he was interrupted by the young queen's crying for her supper, the previous question for which was carried without a negative; and then the house being resumed, the debate was cut short by the impatience of the majority to go and drink her majesty's health. This seeming violence gave occasion to a very long protest, drawn up by sir Archee Mac Sarcasm, in which he contrived to state the claim of the departed fœtus so artfully, that it produced a civil war, and gave rise to those bloody ravages and massacres which so long laid waste the ancient kingdom of Kilkenny, and which were at last terminated by a lucky accident, well known, says my author, to every body, but which he thinks it his duty to relate for the sake of those who never may have heard it. These are his words:

It happened that the archbishop of Tuum (anciently called Meum by the Roman catholic clergy) the great wit of those times, was in the queen-mother's closet, who had the young queen in her lap.[5] His grace was suddenly seized with a violent fit of the cholic, which made him make such wry faces, that the queen-mother thought he was going to die, and ran out of the room to send for a physician, for she was a pattern of goodness, and void of pride. While she was stepped into the servant's hall to call somebody, according to the simplicity of those times, the archbishop's pains encreased, when perceiving something on the mantle-piece, which he took for a peach in brandy, he gulped it all down at once without saying grace, God forgive him, and found great comfort in it. He had not done licking his lips before the queen-mother returned, when queen Grata cried out, "Mama, mama, the gentleman has eat my little brother!" This fortunate event put an end to the contest, the male line entirely failing in the person of the devoured prince. The archbishop, however, who became pope by the name of Innocent the 3^d. having afterwards a son by his sister, named the child Fitzpatrick, as having some of the royal blood in his veins; and from him are descended all the younger branches of the Fitzpatricks of our time. Now the rest of the acts of Grata and all that she did, are they not written in the book of the chronicles of the kings of Kilkenny?

NOTES ON TALE IV.

*This tale was written for Anne Liddel countess of
Ossory, wife of John Fitzpatrick earl of Ossory.
They had a daughter Anne, the subject of this story.*

1 *Vide Lodge's Peerage of Ireland, in the family of Fitzpatrick.*

2 *Queen Anne in her first speech to the parliament said, her heart was entirely
English.*

3 *Lady Ossory had miscarried just then of two sons.*

4 *The housekeeper, as soon as lord Ossory came home, wished him joy of a son
and heir, though both the children were born dead.*

5 *Some commentators have ignorantly supposed that the Irish author is guilty of
a great anachronism in this passage; for having said that the contested succes-
sion occasioned long wars, he yet speaks of queen Grata at the conclusion of
them, as still sitting in her mother's lap as a child. Now I can confute them
from their own state of the question.* Like a child *does not import that she
actually was a child: she only sat* like a child; *and so she might though thirty
years old. Civilians have declared at what period of his life a king may be of
age before he is: but neither Grotius nor Puffendorffe, nor any of the tribe,
have determined how long a king or queen may remain infants after they are
past their infancy.*

Mi Li. A Chinese Fairy Tale

Tale V

M i Li, prince of China, was brought up by his godmother the fairy Hih, who was famous for telling fortunes with a tea-cup. From that unerring oracle she assured him, that he would be the most unhappy man alive unless he married a princess whose name was the same with her father's dominions. As in all probability there could not be above one person in the world to whom that accident had happened, the prince thought there would be nothing so easy as to learn who his destined bride was. He had been too well educated to put the question to his godmother, for he knew when she uttered an oracle, that it was with intention to perplex, not to inform; which has made people so fond of consulting all those who do not give an explicit answer, such as prophets, lawyers, and any body you meet on the road, who, if you ask the way, reply by desiring to know whence you came. Mi Li was no sooner returned to his palace than he sent for his governor, who was deaf and dumb, qualities for which the fairy had selected him, that he might not instil any bad principles into his pupil; however, in recompence, he could talk upon his fingers like an angel. Mi Li asked him directly who the princess was whose name was the same with her father's kingdom? This was a little exaggeration in the prince, but nobody ever repeats any thing just as they heard it: besides, it was excusable in the heir of a great monarchy, who of all things had not been taught to speak truth, and perhaps had never heard what it was. Still it was not the mistake of *kingdom* for *dominions* that puzzled the governor. It never helped him to understand any thing the better for its being rightly stated. However, as he had great presence of mind, which consisted in never giving a direct answer, and in looking as if he could, he replied, it was a question of too great importance to be resolved on a sudden. How came you to know that? said the prince—This youthful impetuosity told the governor that there was something more in the question than he had apprehended; and though he could be very solemn about nothing, he was ten times more so when there was something he did not comprehend. Yet that unknown something occasioning a conflict between his cunning and his ignorance, and the latter being the greater, always betrayed itself, for nothing looks so silly as a fool acting wisdom. The prince repeated his question; the governor demanded why he asked—the prince had not patience to spell the question over again on his fingers, but bawled it as loud as he could to no purpose. The courtiers ran in, and catching up the prince's words, and repeating them imperfectly, it soon flew all over Pekin, and thence into the provinces, and thence into Tartary, and thence to Muscovy, and so on, that the prince wanted to know who the princess was, whose name was the same as her father's. As the Chinese have not the blessing (for aught I know) of having family surnames as we have, and as what would be their christian-names, if they were so happy as to be christians, are quite different for men and women, the Chinese, who think that must be a rule all over the world because it is theirs, decided that there could not exist upon the square face of the earth a woman whose name was the same as her father's. They repeated this so often, and with so much deference and so much obstinacy, that the prince, totally forgetting the original oracle, believed that he wanted to know who the woman was who had the same name as her father. However, remembring there was something in the question that he had taken for royal, he always said *the king her father*. The prime minister consulted the red book or court-calendar, which was *his* oracle, and could find no such princess. All the ministers at foreign courts were instructed to inform themselves if there was any such lady; but as it took up a great deal of time to put these instructions into cypher, the prince's impatience could not wait for the couriers setting out, but he determined to go himself in search of the princess. The old king, who, *as is usual*, had left the whole management of affairs to his son the moment he was fourteen, was charmed with the prince's resolution of seeing the world, which he thought could be done in a few days, the facility of which makes so many monarchs never stir out of their own palaces till it is too late; and his majesty declared, that he should approve of his son's choice, be the lady who she would, provided she answered to the divine designation of having the same name as her father.

The prince rode post to Canton, intending to embark there on board an English man of war. With what infinite transport did he hear the evening before he was to embark, that a sailor knew the identic lady in question. The prince scalded his mouth with the tea he was drinking, broke the old china cup it was in, and which the queen his mother had given him at his departure from Pekin, and which had been given to her great great great great grandmother queen Fi by Confucius himself, and ran down to the vessel and asked for the man who knew his bride. It was honest Tom O'Bull, an Irish sailor, who by his interpreter Mr. James Hall, the supercargo, informed his highness that Mr. Bob Oliver of Sligo had a daughter christened of both his names, the fair miss Bob Oliver.[1] The prince by the plenitude of his power declared Tom a mandarin of the first class, and at Tom's desire promised to speak to his brother the king of Great Ireland, France and Britain, to have him made a peer in his own country, Tom saying he should be ashamed to appear there without being a lord as well as all his acquaintance.

The prince's passion, which was greatly inflamed by Tom's description of her highness Bob's charms, would not let him stay for a proper set of ladies from Pekin to carry to wait on his bride, so he took a dozen of the wives of the first merchants in Canton, and two dozen virgins as maids of honour, who however were disqualified for their employments before his highness got to St. Helena. Tom himself married one of them, but was so great a favourite with the prince, that she still was appointed maid of honour, and with Tom's consent was afterwards married to an English duke.

Nothing can paint the agonies of our royal lover, when on his landing at Dublin he was informed the princess Bob had quitted Ireland, and was married to nobody knew whom. It was well for Tom that he was on Irish ground. He would have been chopped as small as rice, for it is death in China to mislead the heir of the crown through ignorance. To do it knowingly is no crime, any more than in other countries.

As a prince of China cannot marry a woman that has been married before, it was necessary for Mi Li to search the world for another lady equally qualified with miss Bob, whom he forgot the moment he was told he must marry somebody else, and fell equally in love with somebody else, though he knew not with whom. In this suspence he dreamt, *"that he would find his destined spouse, whose father had lost the dominions which never had been his dominions, in a place where there was a bridge over no water, a tomb where nobody ever was buried nor ever would be buried, ruins that were more than they had ever been, a subterraneous passage in which there were dogs with eyes of rubies and emeralds, and a more beautiful menagerie of Chinese pheasants than any in his father's extensive gardens."* This oracle seemed so impossible to be accomplished, that he believed it more than he had done the first, which shewed his great piety. He determined to begin his second search, and being told by the lord lieutenant that there was in England a Mr. Banks,[2] who was going all over the world in search of he did not know what, his highness thought he could not have a better conductor, and sailed for England. There he learnt that the sage Banks was at Oxford, hunting in the Bodleian library for a MS. voyage of a man who had been in the moon, which Mr. Banks thought must have been in the western ocean, where the moon sets, and which planet if he could discover once more, he would take possession of in his majesty's name, upon condition that it should never be taxed, and so be lost again to this country like the rest of his majesty's dominions in that part of the world.

Mi Li took a hired post-chaise for Oxford, but as it was a little rotten it broke on the new road down to Henley. A beggar advised him to walk into general Conway's, who was the most courteous person alive, and would certainly lend him his own chaise. The prince travelled incog. He took the beggar's advice, but going up to the house was told the family were in the grounds, but he should be conducted to them. He was led through a venerable wood of beeches, to a menagerie[3] commanding a more glorious prospect than any in his father's dominions, and full of Chinese pheasants. The prince cried out in extasy, Oh! potent Hih! my dream begins to be accomplished. The gardiner, who knew no Chinese but the names of a few plants, was struck with the similitude of the sounds, but discreetly said not a word. Not finding his lady there, as he expected, he turned back, and plunging suddenly into the thickest gloom of the wood, he descended into a cavern totally dark, the intrepid prince following him boldly. After advancing a great way into this subterraneous vault, at last they perceived light, when on a sudden they were pursued by several small spaniels, and turning to look at them, the prince perceived their eyes[4] shone like emeralds and rubies. Instead of being amazed, as Fo-Hi, the founder of his race, would have been, the prince renewed his exclamations, and cried, I advance! I advance! I shall find my bride! great Hih! thou art infallible! Emerging into light, the imperturbed[5] gardiner conducted his highness to a heap of artificial[6] ruins, beneath which they found a spacious gallery or arcade, where his highness was asked if he would not repose himself; but instead of answering he capered like one frantic, crying out, I advance! I advance! great Hih! I advance!—The gardiner was amazed, and doubted whether he was not conducting a madman to his master and lady, and hesitated whether he should proceed—but as he understood nothing the prince said, and perceiving he must be a foreigner, he concluded he was a Frenchman by his dancing. As the stranger too was so nimble and not at all tired with his walk, the sage gardiner proceeded down a sloping valley, between two mountains cloathed to their summits with cedars, firs, and pines, which he took care to tell the prince were all of his honour the general's own planting: but though the prince had learnt more English in three days in Ireland, than all the French in the world ever learnt in three years, he took no notice of the information, to the great offence of the gardiner, but kept running on, and increased his gambols and exclamations when he perceived the vale was terminated by a stupendous bridge, that seemed composed of the rocks which the giants threw at Jupiter's head, and had not a drop of water beneath[7] it—Where is my bride, my bride? cried Mi Li—I must be near her. The prince's shouts and cries drew a matron from a cottage that stood on a precipice near the bridge, and hung over the river—My lady is down at Ford-house, cried the good[8] woman, who was a little deaf, concluding they had called to her to know. The gardiner knew it was in vain to explain his distress to her, and thought that if the poor gentleman was really mad, his master the general would be the properest person to know how to manage him. Accordingly turning to the left, he led the prince along the banks of the river, which glittered through the opening fallows, while on the other hand a wilderness of shrubs climbed up the pendant cliffs of chalk, and contrasted with the verdant meads and fields of corn beyond the stream. The prince, insensible to such enchanting scenes, galloped wildly along, keeping the poor gardiner on a round trot, till they were stopped by a lonely[9] tomb, surrounded by cypress, yews, and willows, that seemed the monument of some adventurous youth who had been lost in tempting the current, and might have suited the gallant and daring Leander. Here Mi Li first had presence of mind to recollect the little English he knew, and eagerly asked the gardiner whose tomb he beheld before him. It is nobody's—before he could proceed, the prince interrupted him, And will it never be any body's?—Oh! thought the gardiner, now there is no longer any doubt of his phrenzy—and perceiving his master and the family approaching towards them, he endeavoured to get the start, but the prince, much younger, and borne too on the wings of love, set out full speed the moment he saw the company, and particularly a young damsel with them. Running almost breathless up to lady Ailesbury, and seizing miss Campbell's hand—he cried, *Who she? who she?* Lady Ailesbury screamed, the young maiden squalled, the general, cool but offended, rushed between them, and if a prince could be collared, would have collared him—Mi Li kept fast hold with one arm, but pointing to his prize with the other, and with the most eager and supplicating looks intreating for an answer, continued to exclaim, *Who she? who she?* The general perceiving by his accent and manner that he was a foreigner, and rather tempted to laugh than be angry, replied with civil scorn, Why *she* is miss Caroline Campbell, daughter of lord William Campbell, his majesty's late governor of Carolina—Oh, Hih! I now recollect thy words! cried Mi Li—And so she became princess of China.

NOTES ON TALE V.

1 *There really was such a person.*

2 *The gentleman who discovered Otaheite, in company with Dr. Solander.*

3 *Lady Ailesbury's.*

4 *At Park-place there is such a passage cut through a chalk-hill: when dogs are in the middle, the light from the mouth makes their eyes appear in the manner here described.*

5 *Copeland, the gardiner, a very grave person.*

6 *Consequently they seem to have been larger.*

7 *The rustic bridge at Park-place was built by general Conway, to carry the road from Henley, and to leave the communication free between his grounds on each side of the road. Vide last page of 4th. vol. of Anecdotes of Painting.*

8 *The old woman who kept the cottage built by general Conway to command a glorious prospect. Ford-house is a farm house at the termination of the grounds.*

9 *A fictitious tomb in a beautiful spot by the river, built for a point of view: it has a small pyramid on it.*

A True Love Story

Tale VI

In the height of the animosities between the factions of the Guelfs and Ghibellines, a party of Venetians had made an inroad into the territories of the Viscontis, sovereigns of Milan, and had carried off the young Orondates, then at nurse. His family were at that time under a cloud, though they could boast of being descended from Canis Scaliger, lord of Verona. The captors sold the beautiful Orondates to a rich widow of the noble family of Grimaldi, who having no children, brought him up with as much tenderness as if he had been her son. Her fondness increased with the growth of his stature and charms, and the violence of his passions were augmented by the signora Grimaldi's indulgence. Is it necessary to say that love reigned predominantly in the soul of Orondates? Or that in a city like Venice a form like that of Orondates met with little resistance?

The Cyprian queen, not content with the numerous oblations of Orondates on her altars, was not satisfied while his heart remained unengaged. Across the canal, overagainst the palace of Grimaldi, stood a convent of Carmelite nuns, the abbess of which had a young African slave of the most exquisite beauty, called Azora, a year younger than Orondates. Jet and japan were tawny and without lustre, when compared to the hue of Azora. Afric never produced a female so perfect as Azora; as Europe could boast but of one Orondates.

The signora Grimaldi, though no bigot, was pretty regular at her devotions, but as lansquenet was more to her taste than praying, she hurried over her masses as fast as she could, to allot more of her precious time to cards. This made her prefer the church of the Carmelites, separated only by a small bridge, though the abbess was of a contrary faction. However, as both ladies were of equal quality, and had had no altercations that could countenance incivility, reciprocal curtsies always passed between them, the coldness of which each pretended to lay on their attention to their devotions, though the signora Grimaldi attended but little to the priest, and the abbess was chiefly employed in watching and criticising the inattention of the signora.

Not so Orondates and Azora. Both constantly accompanied their mistresses to mass, and the first moment they saw each other was decisive in both breasts. Venice ceased to have more than one fair in the eyes of

Orondates, and Azora had not remarked till then that there could be more beautiful beings in the world than some of the Carmelite nuns.

The seclusion of the abbess, and the aversion between the two ladies, which was very cordial on the side of the holy one, cut off all hopes from the lovers. Azora grew grave and pensive and melancholy; Orondates surly and intractable. Even his attachment to his kind patroness relaxed. He attended her reluctantly but at the hours of prayer. Often did she find him on the steps of the church ere the doors were opened. The signora Grimaldi was not apt to make observations. She was content with indulging her own passions, seldom restrained those of others; and though good offices rarely presented themselves to her imagination, she was ready to exert them when applied to, and always talked charitably of the unhappy at her cards, if it was not a very unlucky deal.

Still it is probable that she never would have discovered the passion of Orondates, had not her woman, who was jealous of his favour, given her a hint; at the same time remarking, under affectation of good will, how well the circumstances of the lovers were suited, and that as her ladyship was in years, and would certainly not think of providing for a creature she had bought in the public market, it would be charitable to marry the fond couple, and settle them on her farm in the country.

Fortunately madame Grimaldi always was open to good impressions, and rarely to bad. Without perceiving the malice of her woman, she was struck with the idea of a marriage. She loved the cause, and always promoted it when it was honestly in her power. She seldom made difficulties, and never apprehended them. Without even examining Orondates on the state of his inclinations, without recollecting that madame Capello and she were of different parties, without taking any precautions to guard against a refusal, she instantly wrote to the abbess to propose a marriage between Orondates and Azora.

The latter was in madame Capello's chamber when the note arrived. All the fury that authority loves to console itself with for being under restraint, all the asperity of a bigot, all the acrimony of party, and all the fictitious rage that prudery adopts when the sensual enjoyments of others are concerned, burst out on the helpless Azora, who was unable to divine how she was concerned in the fatal letter. She was made to endure all the calumnies that the abbess would have been glad to have hurled at the head of madame Grimaldi, if her own character and the rank of that offender would have allowed it. Impotent menaces of revenge were repeated with emphasis, and as nobody in the convent dared to contradict her, she gratified her anger and love of prating with endless tautologies. In fine, Azora was strictly locked up and bread and water were ordered as sovereign cures for love. Twenty replies to madame Grimaldi were written and torn, as not sufficiently expressive of a resentment that was rather vociferous than eloquent, and her confessor was at last forced to write one, in which he prevailed to have some holy cant inserted, though forced to compound for a heap of irony that related to the antiquity of her family, and for many unintelligible allusions to vulgar stories which the Ghibelline party had treasured up against the Guelfs. The most lucid part of the epistle pronounced a sentence of eternal chastity on Azora, not without some sarcastic expressions against the promiscuous amours of Orondates, which ought in common decorum to have banished him long ago from the mansion of a widowed matron.

Just as this fulminatory mandate had been transcribed and signed by the lady abbess in full chapter, and had been consigned to the confessor to deliver, the portress of the convent came running out of breath, and announced to the venerable assembly, that Azora, terrified by the abbess's blows and threats, had fallen in labour and miscarried of four puppies: for be it known to all posterity, that Orondates was an Italian greyhound, and Azora a black spaniel.

The Bird's Nest

Supplemental Tale *

Guzalme, Queen of Serendip, was reposing in the Pavilion of Odours on a couch made of Down from the wings of butterflies, when a Voice that could be heard only in a Dream, said look! look! She turned her head, without opening her eyes, &

---

*Not included in the Strawberry Hill *Hieroglyphic Tales,* this tale is reproduced from a handwritten copy entitled "Hieroglyphic Tales, Tale the Fifth." [Ed.]

saw a few paces from the Window a tree of transparent rosewood, that produced vast bunches of white China cups & saucers, which cast a perfume like the breath of the Houries. On one of the upper branches appeared a bird's nest, composed of shreds of mignionette, trolly, & Brussels lace. Impatient to see what the Nest contained, She climbed up the tree, without stirring off her couch, when happening to touch a flageolet that lay under the nest, it immediately sung an Italian air beginning, Vita dell' alma mia. The Queen could have listened forever to the silver notes, but a large bud on a neighbouring bough blowing at the same instant, & disclosing itself into the Shape of a heart-looking-glass, She was transported to see herself a thousand times handsomer than ever, tho She was before more beautifull than Azrouz, Solomon's favourite Mistress. Concluding this wonderfull flower was a present from Heaven, She thought it would be a sin ever to cease looking in it, & accordingly adjusting herself into the most languishing posture She could contrive, She determined to remain in that position for ever. She had scarce taken this pious resolution, when She heard a violent chattering of teeth, & strange inarticulate sounds. Casting down her eyes towards the ground, She beheld a vast Vermilion Baboon, as least ten feet high, who, for She had forgot that She stood on a very high branch, & that there was a good deal of wind, seemed to be eagerly gazing at her garters that were set with eyes of Turtle Doves, & made a kind of amorous twilight within the circle of her surrounding garments. Never was a Situation so critically sentimental as her Majesty's. If She climbed higher, as her first thought directed, She would but expose her person still farther. If She leaped down, the Danger was yet greater. What could She do? Nothing but what a Woman always does in critical cases—that is, nothing. She was sure She had had no ill intention—Fortune was to blame, & could She govern Fortune? Determining therefore not to be accessory to whatever might happen, She resolved to forget that the Baboon was there; but as it is one's Duty to contribute all in one's power to convince a lover that he has no hopes, & as nothing can put even a disagreeable Lover out of one's head, except thinking on one's self, She set herself with increase of earnestness to look again in the marvellous glass, but She found it much more difficult to please herself with an Attitude. She changed her position so often, that the Baboon, who was an excellent Mimic, could not help imitating her, so that every bird in the forest laughed till it cried again. She was going to be angry, but a watch made of a grain of millet which She wore in her ear, happening to strike Six, instead of the Baboon She beheld at the foot of the Tree a venerable Man, clothed with white robes made of seed pearl that fell down to his feet; & that were gathered round his waste by a girdle of Emeralds set like fig leaves, but the clasp was quite worn out it had been unbuckled so often, for He bathed in the Euphrates seven times every day, & he was now five thousand nine hundred & thirteen years old. Addressing himself to the Queen, he said, Bright Star of the morning, Dispel your fears; in me behold the Patriarch Abraham! Ld bless me! said She, & how came you here? When I was conveyed from this World, replied He, by Azuriel the Angel of Death, as he was carrying my Soul to Heaven, a Voice from this Forest, cried out, oh you old Villain, was not it enough to leave me & my poor babe Ishmael to starve in this Desart, but do you think you shall go to heaven too without me! Azuriel, continued She, I insist upon your taking me along with that Deceiver—Dear Madam, said the Angel, that is impossible—Somehow or other Sarah has got thither before you, & there will be no living in peace if you should meet. All I can do for you is This. Abraham shall one day in every week wander about this desart with you for twelve hours—but as you will not be the better for his company since he will be nothing but Soul, & as Sarah will still make a racket if She sees him with you in his human form, He shall take the Shape of any Animal he pleases—& this metamorphosis he must submit to, till a more beautifull Woman than you, with the finest Shape, the blackest eyes, & the reddest lips in the world, shall come a-Bird's-nesting in this forest. I have now, continued Abraham to the Queen, undergone this penance above five thousand years, without any hopes of being relieved from it till a quarter of an hour ago, when I saw you sleeping in the Pavilion of Odours. It was I who whispered to you to look at this tree, & the Event has answered my Expectation. I have seen a Woman more beautifull than Hagar—nay, Madam, do not blush—& you will see the Bird of Solomon—Look! Look!—The Queen hearing a chirping over her head, cast up her eyes, & within the nest on a white satten quilt fringed with Diamonds & turquoises She saw a little purple fig made of a link Amethyst, It had a bullfinch's head of ruby & jet, a bill of topaz, & a tail of peacock's feathers, flounced with rainbows. This dear little Creature, which was thirty times Less than the smallest hummingbird, sat upon two Ostrich's eggs of Opal,—which was not at all extraordinary, for everthing that belonged to Solomon had the gift of dilating itself to any Magnitude; & it was as easy for the Sweet little Creature to extend itself over two Ostrich's Eggs, as it is to make a million of people drunk with a single glass of Champagne, which may be soon effected if you can but get them into a wilderness where there is not a drop of wine, for all the Difficulty of committing a Miracle consists in the Impossibility: any body might perform one if it were possible. On one of the Eggs were strange Characters, on the other, in Hebrew letters, were the Words, Oroknoz Alapol. For heavens sake, cried Guzalme, tell me the meaning of those Words: there must be some Wonderfull virtue in them. They are the names of a great Philosopher, said Abram, who is wiser than Solomon, & writes more nonsense. The Characters you do not understand are in the language of a Western Island, & signify the same as Oroknoz Alapol, which being interpreted, is, the Leanest of true Believers. He will fall in Love with you, & will write fairy Tales for your Entertainment— but give me yr hand, & let me help you down—Stay a minute, said She, I will only get a few Seeds of this looking-glass flower, it is the whitest I ever saw; I will have them raised in my green-house, & furnish all my rooms with them. Having said those words, She stretched out her arm to gather the flower, but her foot slipping, She fell down—and waked.

Postscript

The foregoing Tales are given for no more than they are worth: they are mere whimsical trifles, written chiefly for private entertainment, and for private amusement half a dozen copies only are printed. They deserve at most to be considered as an attempt to vary the stale and beaten class of stories and novels, which, though works of invention, are almost always devoid of imagination. It would scarcely be credited, were it not evident from the Bibliotheque des Romans, which contains the fictitious adventures that have been written in all ages and all countries, that there should have been so little fancy, so little variety, and so little novelty, in writings in which the imagination is fettered by no rules, and by no obligation of speaking truth. There is infinitely more invention in history, which has no merit if devoid of truth, than in romances and novels, which pretend to none.

FINIS.

Editorial: Thomas Christensen, David Peattie,
Kirsten Janene-Nelson
Design: Sharon Smith, San Francisco
Illustrations and hand lettering:
Jill McElmurry, Dunsmuir, California
Typesetting: Katherine Gibbon, San Francisco
Printing and binding: Data Reproductions,
Rochester Hills, Michigan

◆

The typeface is Adobe Caslon, possibly the most faithful of modern Caslon typefaces to the originals designed and cut by William Caslon in the mid-1700s. Typographer Robert Bringhurst termed Caslon "the epitome of the English Baroque." Last of the Old-Style faces, its popularity was eventually superceded by the "transitional" typefaces of another eighteenth-century English type designer, John Baskerville. Nonetheless, it was a favorite of Horace Walpole at his Strawberry Hill Press and was used by him in his original edition of *Hieroglyphic Tales*.